O9-AIG-328

To my wonderful sister Karin who never forgets a birthday and every day deserves a parade. —E.O.

For June Gregory, the world's best Nana, baker, and birthday mess maker. —J.T.

BIGFOOT does NOT like BIRTHDAY PARTIES

Written by Eric Ode
Illustrated by Jaime Temairik

little bigfoot
an imprint of sasquatch books
seattle, wa

Today is Bigfoot's birthday.

All the people of Mossy Pockets
are coming together to celebrate.
Everyone will be at the party—
everyone except Bigfoot because . . .

Here comes the mayor in his fancy suit.
Doesn't he look grand?

And now here comes the marching band—
the clarinet, the sousaphone,
the piccolo, the baritone,
the trombone player, the girl with the flute.
They follow the mayor in his fancy suit
all through the town.

It's Bigfoot's birthday party!

Here comes the baker.
Her arms are piled high with pies—
cherry pies, berry pies,
lemon, apple, and creamy
maple pies.

The baker follows the
marching band.

Step aside! Here they come!
The man who plays the big bass drum;
the clarinet; the saxophone;

the sassy, brassy baritone;
the trombone player; the girl with the flute—
they follow the mayor in his fancy suit
up the town's main street.

And now here come all the rest—
the cowboy in his boots and vest,
the lady with the purple hat,
the circus clown, the acrobat.

It's Bigfoot's
birthday party!

They all march up the street
and up the hill
until . . .

the mayor stops and raises his hand.

Everyone is silent:
the boys and girls,
the marching band;
they all wait and listen.
And then . . .
Grrrrr. Grrrrr.
"Do you hear that?"
asks the mayor.
"Is that Bigfoot?"

GRRR GRR

No, it isn't Bigfoot. Bigfoot does not like birthday parties.

"It's only a dog," says the girl with the flute
to the mayor in his fancy suit.
"A lazy dog who sleeps on a log and snores."

RR GRRRRRrr

SSSSSSS SSSSSSS SSSSSSS

Sssssss. Sssssss.

"What's that?" asks the man
with the big bassoon.
"Is that Bigfoot?"

No, it isn't Bigfoot. Bigfoot does not like
birthday parties.

"It's only a snake," says the boy
with the yellow balloon
to the man who plays the big bassoon.
"A snake who stays behind a stone
and watches the dog
who sleeps on a log and snores."

SSSSS SSSSS

GRRRP! GRR

Grrrrp, grrrp!
"Over there," says the lady with the purple hat.
"Is that Bigfoot?"

No, it isn't Bigfoot. Bigfoot still does not like birthday parties.

"It's only a frog," says the acrobat
to the lady with the purple hat.
"A grumpy frog who lives in the lake
and hides from the snake
who stays by the stone
and watches the dog
who sleeps on a log and snores."

BZZZZ BZZZZZZ

Bzzzzzz. Bzzzzzz.
"What's that?" asks the baker.
"Is that Bigfoot?"

NO, it isn't Bigfoot, because, as we all know,
Bigfoot does not like birthday parties.

"It's only a fly," says the mayor.
"Yes, it's only a fly," says the trombone player.
"It's only a fly," the people sigh.
A fuzzy fly who buzzes by
and startles the frog who swims alone
and hides from the snake who stays by the stone
and watches the dog
who sleeps on a log and snores.

ZZ BZZZ BZZZ BZZZ

Zip!
The fly darts past the mayor.
"Shoo!" says the mayor.

The snake sees the frog.

"Sssssss," says the snake from behind the stone.

He chases the frog
who hopped from the lake
to catch the fly
that buzzes by.

Buzz!
The fly does a loopty-loop around the big bass drum.
The frog watches the fuzzy fly dart about.

GRRRP!

"Grrrp!" says the frog.
He hops from the lake to chase the fly.

WOOF!

Now the dog sees the snake.
"Woof!" says the dog.
He jumps from the log
and chases the snake
who left the stone
to chase the frog who swam alone
and hopped from the lake
to catch the fly that buzzes by.

And then the fly sees the pies.
He sees the cherry pies and berry pies.
He sees the lemon, apple, and creamy maple pies.

"He sees the pies!" shouts the lady with the purple hat.

"He sees the pies!" hollers the acrobat.

"He sees the pies!" yells the trombone player.

"STOP THAT FLY!" shouts the mayor.

The mayor jumps up to catch the fly.
Up goes the mayor!

And, what a surprise!

DOWN GOES the MAYOR;

UP GO the PIES!

They fly through the air,
 and they come back down.
They fall on the frog and the dog and the clown.
They fall on the baker; they fall on the mayor,
 the man with the drum, and the trombone player.

What a sight! Pies everywhere!

Pies on the man with the
big bassoon.
Pies on the boy with the
yellow balloon.
Pies on the acrobat
dressed in red.
Pies on the snake and . . .

on Bigfoot's head!

Does Bigfoot snarl?
Does Bigfoot scowl?
Does Bigfoot gripe or grunt or growl?
No, Bigfoot grins,
and then he giggles—
laughs so loud
the forest jiggles.

Then everyone smiles
and uncovers their ears.
And everyone dances,
and everyone cheers.

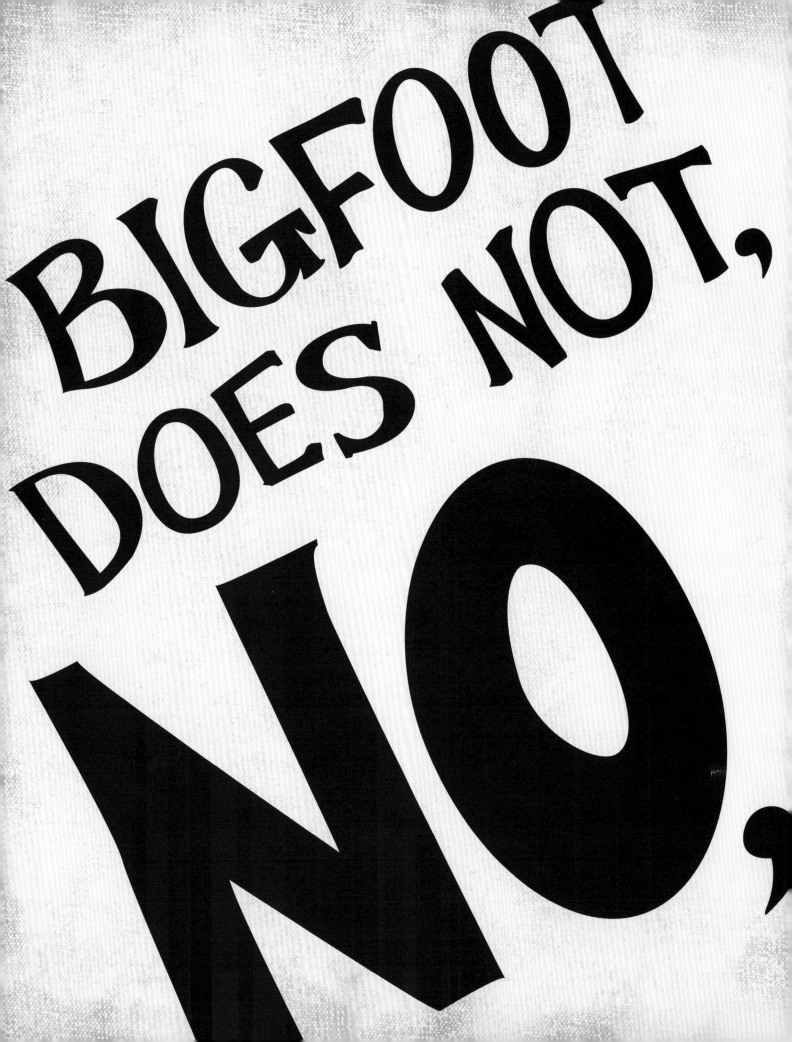

HE ABSOLUTELY does NOT like BIRTHDAY PARTIES!

But did you know,
or did you guess?

Bigfoot loves a birthday mess!

Copyright © 2015 by Eric Ode
Illustrations copyright © 2015 by Jaime Temairik

All rights reserved. No portion of this book may be
reproduced or utilized in any form, or by any electronic,
mechanical, or other means, without the prior written
permission of the publisher.

Manufactured in China by C&C Offset Printing Co. Ltd.
Shenzhen, Guangdong Province,
in June 2015

Published by Little Bigfoot,
an imprint of Sasquatch Books

20 19 18 17 16 15   9 8 7 6 5 4 3 2 1

Editor: Tegan Tigani
Production editors: Nancy W. Cortelyou
and Emma Reh
Illustrations: Jaime Temairik

Library of Congress Cataloging-in-Publication
Data is available.

ISBN: 978-1-63217-004-0

Sasquatch Books
1904 Third Avenue, Suite 710
Seattle, WA 98101
(206) 467-4300
www.sasquatchbooks.com
custserv@sasquatchbooks.com

P9-DHS-589

BALLOON ON THE MOON

Dan McCann

Illustrated by **Nathan Hale**

Walker & Company New York

To Jake, Will & Lizzie—my inspirations;
to Sharon—my hero;
to Kelly—my everything
—D. M.

To Pluto, we hardly knew you
—N. H.

Text copyright © 2008 by Dan McCann
Illustrations copyright © 2008 by Nathan Hale

All rights reserved. No part of this book may be reproduced or transmitted in any form or by any means,
electronic or mechanical, including photocopying, recording, or by any information storage
and retrieval system, without permission in writing from the publisher.

First published in the United States of America in 2008 by Walker Publishing Company, Inc.
Distributed to the trade by Macmillan

For information about permission to reproduce selections from this book, write to
Permissions, Walker & Company, 175 Fifth Avenue, New York, New York 10010

Library of Congress Cataloging-in-Publication Data
McCann, Dan.
Balloon on the moon / by Dan McCann ; illustrated by Nathan Hale.
p.   cm.
Summary: When his little brother's red balloon goes flying off into the sky, six-and-three-quarters-year-old
Jake goes on a mission to the moon to retrieve it for him, because that is what big brothers are for.
ISBN-13: 978-0-8027-8092-8 • ISBN-10: 0-8027-8092-X (hardcover)
ISBN-13: 978-0-8027-8093-5 • ISBN-10: 0-8027-8093-8 (reinforced)
[1. Brothers—Fiction. 2. Balloons—Fiction. 3. Lost and found possessions—Fiction.
4. Space flight to the moon—Fiction.] I. Hale, Nathan, ill. II. Title.
PZ7.M1241Bal 2008   [E]—dc22   2007032180

Typeset in ITC Bauhaus Medium
The art for this book was created using Golden Acrylics on Crescent board and Adobe Photoshop.

Visit Walker & Company's Web site at www.walkeryoungreaders.com

Printed in Malaysia
2 4 6 8 10 9 7 5 3 1 (hardcover)
2 4 6 8 10 9 7 5 3 1 (reinforced)

All papers used by Walker & Company are natural, recyclable products
made from wood grown in well-managed forests. The manufacturing processes
conform to the environmental regulations of the country of origin.

Daddy was quick but not quick enough. A gust of wind caught Will's red balloon and swept it skyward. Daddy jumped for the string, but it was no use.

Soon the balloon was off, off, off—nothing
but a small red dot in the clear blue sky.

"I'm sorry, Will," said Daddy. "It looks like
it's off to the moon."

Will started to cry, which made Jake, his
big brother, very sad.

Lying in his bed that night, Jake thought about how much Will loved that balloon. Just before he dozed off, a wild idea came to him. Yes, he decided that's what he had to do.

Accomplishing this most important mission
required a trip to the Kennedy Space Center, NASA's
launch headquarters. While his mom looked at a
rocket model, Jake headed for the front counter.

"One ticket to the moon, please," he said
politely.

"How old are you?" asked the woman behind
the counter.

"I'm six and three-quarters," said Jake proudly.

"Just a minute," said the woman. She picked up
the phone and spoke in a whisper. Moments later,
a man in a dark blue suit came out.

"So," said the man in the dark blue suit, "I hear you want to be an astronaut."

"My brother's balloon flew to the moon," said Jake. "I'm going to get it for him."

The man in the dark blue suit looked hard at the boy.

"I won't take up much space," Jake continued. "I don't even have to eat. Well, maybe just a snack or two . . ."

"You've got spunk," the man replied. "I like that. The next mission leaves tomorrow at eight."

"I'll be there," said Jake with a smile, "as long as my mom and dad say it's okay."

"Of course," said the man in the dark blue suit. "Welcome aboard . . . as long as your mom and dad say it's okay."

Jake's mom and dad really weren't too thrilled with the idea of their oldest son hurtling through space—especially since he was only six and three-quarters. But they agreed when they saw how sad Will was without his red balloon and how determined Jake was to help.

Jake was back at the space center at seven o'clock sharp the next morning. A mob of reporters and photographers was there, asking question after question.

"Are you nervous?"

"Do you like Tang?"

"Shouldn't you be in school?"

The time came for Jake to say good-bye to his family.

"Let's get you suited up," said the man in dark blue.

A team of men and women put Jake into his specially fitted space suit. They slid his hands into special gloves and snapped on his helmet.

Inside the rocket, a booster seat was waiting. The crew strapped Jake in tightly. His nervous stomach was doing flips. To make matters worse, he had forgotten to go to the bathroom. It was too late now.

4

"Let's go get that red balloon," said the commander.

The booster rockets roared to life.

"Godspeed, Jake," said a voice from mission control.

On went the countdown:

three...

two...

one...

BLASTOFF!

"Bye-bye, Jake," Will yelled from below.

The engines were loud. The ride was bumpy—bumpier than any roller coaster.

"How are you doing, Jake?" asked the commander as they shot spaceward.

"Can't talk," he replied, trying hard not to toss his cookies.

Jake grabbed his armrests and took a deep
breath. Then, before he knew it, the bumping
stopped. The rocket had arrived in outer space.
　　His cookies intact, Jake unfastened his seat belt
and slipped off his helmet. It began to float . . .
and so did he.

"Whoa," said Jake quietly, "I'm flying."

Excitement erupted as he "swam" to the window.
"I'm flying, oh yeah! I'm flying, oh yeah!"
Jake did a few flips on the way, then he stopped
to gaze outside. What an amazing view!
"Is that . . . ," he began.
"That's Mother Earth," said the commander.
"That's where we live—and where the people who
love us live."

Jake's smile melted away. Suddenly he missed his mom, dad, and brother. He missed his bedroom and his toys. He had to remind himself he was on a mission—a most important one.

"You must be hungry," said the commander.

Jake remembered saying that he wouldn't eat anything, but he was starving. He gobbled up a hot dog, which was pretty cold, and some astronaut ice cream, which wasn't. He washed it all down with a pouch of Tang.

After dinner, Jake drifted into a peaceful sleep. Making history can be tiring, especially when you have to wake up at six o'clock in the morning to do it.

By the time Jake woke, the rocket was orbiting the moon.

"Jake!" called the commander. "It's time."

The boy astronaut made his way to the lunar module, which, after a quick descent, landed softly on the moon.

"You are 'Go' for moonwalk," said mission control. "Good luck, Jake."

Jake carefully climbed down the ladder and onto the lunar surface.

"That's one small step for a little man," said Jake, "one giant leap for childkind."

Jake looked around. It was so quiet. He squinted his eyes, and there, tangled among some moon rocks, he saw it—his brother's red balloon, along with a collection of wayward kites and some other lost toys. His stomach jumped with excitement.

"I'm going for capture," said Jake.

He bounced over to the rocks and swiftly snagged Will's balloon. He grabbed a couple of kites as well.

"Someone on Earth is probably missing you."

Jake planted an American flag in the soil and wrote a "J" and a "W" with his gloved finger. Then he made his way back to the lunar module— mission accomplished.

The crew let out a great cheer.

"Hooray for Jake!" they shouted.

"Mission control," said the commander, "we're coming home."

"Can we swing by the North Pole?" asked Jake.

"Negative," said the commander.

The reentry into Earth's atmosphere was no picnic. Jake was very hot in his flight suit, and his stomach was queasy. But the splashdown was perfect.

After the helicopter brought Jake in, the reporters and photographers were waiting.

"Did you see any moon people?"

"How does it feel to be the youngest astronaut in history?"

"Did you toss your cookies?"

Most important, they asked, "Did you find your brother's balloon?"

Jake proudly held it up for the crowd to see.

NJH076

Jake was happy to have met so many nice people, happy to have flown into orbit, and happy to have walked on the moon. But seeing his brother's face when he brought back his red balloon—that made him happiest of all.

"Thank you, Jake," said Will.

"You're welcome, Will," said Jake. "That's what big brothers are for."